~~STANLEY~~ LioNel GOES APE

BY GRIFF

ticktock MEDIA

for Rachel, my little big sister...(x)
("...is she a frog you found in the bog?...")

First published in Great Britain in 2001.
Copyright © *ticktock* Entertainment Ltd 2002.
Century Place, Lamberts Road, Tunbridge Wells, Kent, TN2 3EH.

Text and Illustrations © Andrew Griffin 2001
ISBN 1 86007 299 2
Printed in China
A CIP catalogue record for this book is available from the British Library.

This is Stanley. Stanley *looks* like an ordinary little boy, but his mum thinks he's a monkey.

In fact,
she calls him a **cheeky** monkey...

a mucky pup,

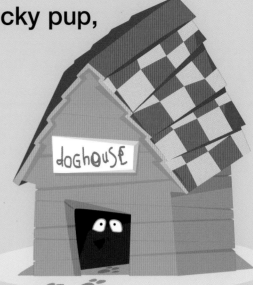

doGhouse

or a clumsy hippo.

But mostly she calls
him a cheeky monkey.

Stanley isn't so sure.

Stanley knows _everything_ there is to know about monkeys and apes.

They have lots of hair... unlike Stanley.

They usually walk on all fours... unlike Stanley.

They are great climbers... unlike Stanley.

They also have smaller brains.

Stanley thinks this sounds more like Lionel.

INGREDIENTS:
water (50%), sugar (25%),
caffeine (10%), nE1'sGES (5%),
stabilizers (4%), artificial milk flavouring (3.5%),
artificial banana flavouring (2.4%),
cow's milk (trace), banana fruit extract (trace)

NUTRITION INFORMATION:
typical values per carton
Energy   3000kcal
Protein   trace
Carbohydrate   trace
Fat   300g
Fibre   trace
Sodium   205g

BANANA-MILK

Lionel is Stanley's **big** brother.

If Stanley is a monkey,
then Lionel must be an ape!

He climbs like an ape.

He swings from trees, just like an ape.

He can spend half the day eating and
the other half sleeping, just like an ape!

Lionel even *looks* a bit like an ape!

He has long dangly arms like a *gibbon*, and even walks a bit like one!

He has sticky-out ears and pulls funny faces like a *chimpanzee*.

But if Lionel *were* an ape, which one would he be?

A **chimpanzee?**

Lionel is as crazy as a chimpanzee
and loves playing around.

But chimps are good at using tools to help them eat.

Lionel makes a mess with a knife and fork!

Maybe Lionel is more like...

A gorilla?

They are very big and very strong.

But gorillas are vegetarians
and eat masses of greens every day.

Lionel won't touch
his greens, no matter
how hard Mum tries.

Maybe Lionel is more like...

An **orang-utan?**

They are great climbers and love to just hang around.

But orang-utans make their own treetop nests every night.

Lionel can't even make his own bed!
Maybe Lionel is more like...

A gibbon?

Lionel is as noisy as a gibbon.

But gibbons are the smallest of the apes.

Stanley thinks Lionel is **huge.**

Sometimes...

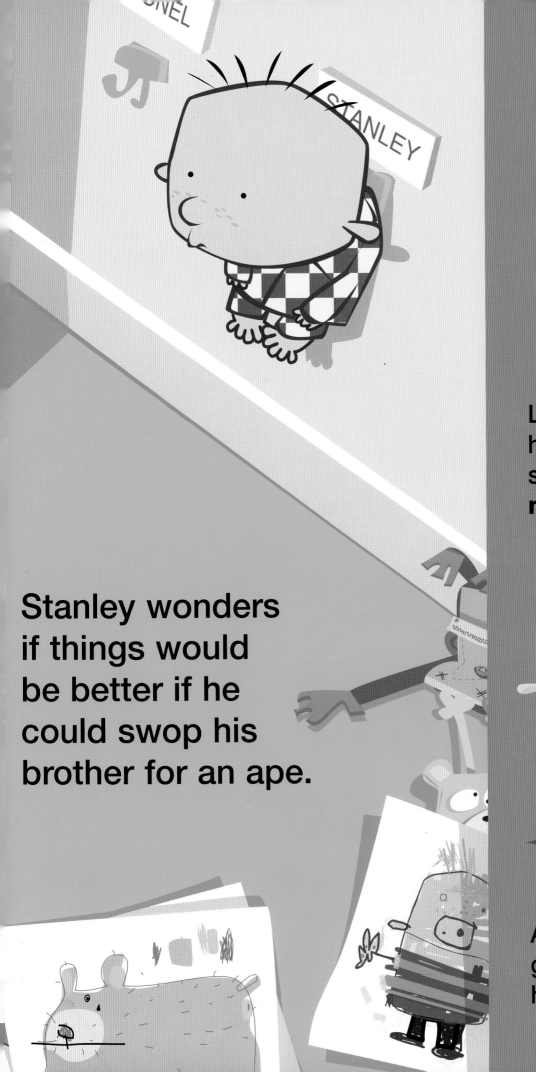

Stanley wonders if things would be better if he could swop his brother for an ape.

Lionel always hides tasty snacks and **never** shares.

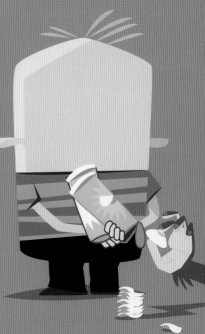

Apes are very good at finding hidden food...

And are happy to share!

Lionel is often **very** grumpy!

Apes can be very friendly...

And *love* to groom each other!

Stanley hates wearing Lionel's hand-me-down clothes.

With an ape, he wouldn't have to...

Apes don't **wear** any clothes!

Stanley changes
his mind.

Who needs a stinky old ape when you can have a stinky **big** brother?

And besides...

Some apes are even **bigger** and *stinkier* than Lionel!